You can be a
Brownie Girl Scout, too!

If you are 6, 7, or 8 years old, or in the 1st, 2nd, or 3rd grade, just ask your parents to look in your local telephone directory under "Girl Scouts," and call for information. You can also ask your parents to call **Girl Scouts of the U.S.A.** at **1-(212) 852-8000** or write to 420 Fifth Avenue, New York, NY 10018-2702 to find out about becoming a Girl Scout in your area.

In fond memory of
Lynne P. Griggs—J.O'C.

To Laura—L.S.L.

This publication may not be reproduced, stored in a retrieval system, or transmitted in whole or in part or by any means, electronic or mechanical, photocopying, recording, or otherwise, without the prior written consent of Girl Scouts of the United States of America, 420 Fifth Avenue, New York, NY 10018-2702.

Copyright © 1994 by Girl Scouts of the United States of America. All rights reserved. Published by Grosset & Dunlap, Inc., a member of The Putnam & Grosset Group, New York, in cooperation with Girl Scouts of the United States of America. GROSSET & DUNLAP is a trademark of Grosset & Dunlap, Inc. Published simultaneously in Canada. Printed in the U.S.A.

Library of Congress Cataloging-in-Publication Data

O'Connor, Jane.
    Think, Corrie, think! / by Jane O'Connor ; illustrated by Laurie Struck Long.
      p.   cm.—(Here come the Brownies! ; 5)
    Summary: When she is teamed up with the smartest girl in second grade to work on a Thinking Day project for Brownies, Corrie learns that friends can be different from each other.
    [1. Girl Scouts—Fiction.   2. Friendship—Fiction.]   I. Long, Laurie Struck, ill.
II. Title.   III. Series.
PZ7.0222Th   1994
[Fic]—dc20   93-41214

ISBN 0-448-40465-6 (pbk.)   A B C D E F G H I J

ISBN 0-448-40466-4 (GB)   A B C D E F G H I J

HERE COME THE BROWNIES

A Brownie Girl Scout Book

Think, Corrie, Think!

By Jane O'Connor
Illustrated by Laurie Struck Long

Grosset & Dunlap • New York
In association with GIRL SCOUTS OF THE U.S.A.

1

"*¡Ay bendito!*" said Corrie. That meant "Oh my goodness!" in Spanish. She took the spelling paper from her teacher, Mrs. Fujikawa. Then she slunk down in her seat. She'd missed four words on this week's test. Four out of ten! That was the worst she'd ever done.

Spelling was not Corrie's favorite subject. Corrie's favorite was art. In art, all she had to do was use her imagination. But imagination didn't count on spelling tests. In spelling, it didn't matter if you got things *almost* right. Every letter had to be perfect—or it was *all* wrong.

Corrie sneaked a peek at her neighbor, Krissy A. She couldn't help but see that Krissy A. had gotten every word right. Even *stomach*.

But that was hardly news. Krissy A. was the smartest kid in 2-B. She was a whiz at math, and she was in the highest reading group—while Corrie had to leave the classroom twice a week for "Special Reading."

What was it like having such a big brain? Corrie wondered. Did it ever give Krissy a headache?

Mrs. Fujikawa liked to mix up the desks in 2-B every once in a while. So for two weeks now Corrie had been sitting next to Krissy A. Still, Corrie had trouble thinking of stuff to say besides "hi." It was like her tongue got all frozen. Funny, because Corrie usually found it pretty easy to make friends. The trouble was Krissy was so serious and quiet. The only time she really spoke up was in class when Mrs. Fujikawa called on her. And then Krissy always had the right answer.

Corrie sighed and stashed her spelling paper in her going-home folder. At least it was Friday. And Friday meant Brownies! Her Brownie Girl Scout troop always met in the lunchroom right after school.

Corrie couldn't wait.

At last the bell rang. Kids scrambled for coats and bookbags. In the rush to the doorway, Corrie and Krissy A. bumped into each other.

"Oops! Sorry," they both said at the same time.

If it had been Amy or Marsha, Corrie would have swept out her arm and said, "After you, my dear!" in a fancy lady voice. But she didn't. Krissy A. would probably think she was just being silly.

"Move it, Corrie! You're going to be late for Brownies," Amy called from out in the hall.

Corrie looked at Krissy A. Krissy was in the troop, too. But she was just standing there, zipping up her bookbag. "Come on, Krissy. Walk with us," Corrie said.

Krissy smiled and followed Corrie. They joined Lauren, Marsha, Krissy S., Sarah, and Amy, the other girls from 2-B who were going to the troop meeting.

"Hey, Corrie!" Amy yanked on Corrie's backpack. "What's purple and hairy and has sixteen legs?"

Amy was always telling jokes Corrie had never heard before. But at last! Here was one she knew!

"I don't know," said Corrie, acting scared. "But whatever it is, it's crawling up your neck!" She ran her fingers up Amy's neck like a wiggly spider. Amy squealed, much to Corrie's satisfaction.

"Hey! I've got one," said Marsha. "My brother told me this one."

Soon everybody was trading jokes. But when Amy poked Krissy A. and said, "Your turn, Krissy," Krissy looked almost frightened, the way other kids looked when they got caught not knowing an answer in class.

"Um, I can't think of one right now," she said, reddening.

"No big deal," Amy told her. Then she broke into a run down the hallway.

Corrie followed, and as soon as she spotted the sign outside the lunchroom that said "BROWNIE MEETING INSIDE," she felt her bad mood disappearing. It was always that way with Brownies.

Corrie had moved into town only six months ago. But right away the Brownies had welcomed her. Now she had lots of friends. Corrie didn't even feel like a new kid anymore.

After snack was over, the whole troop sat on the floor in a circle. Corrie really liked the Brownie Ring. That was when they planned things and made decisions.

"Today we're going to talk about a special day that's coming up," said Mrs. Q. Mrs. Q. was their troop leader. "It's called Thinking Day."

"I hope that doesn't mean we have to keep thinking all day long," Amy said. "Because my poor brain couldn't take it."

Mrs. Q. laughed with the rest of the girls. "You were a Brownie last year, Amy. So I know you know all about Thinking Day."

Mrs. Q. looked around the circle. "But for our new girls, Thinking Day is the day Girl Scouts and Girl Guides all over the world 'think about' each other and how the spirit of friendship brings all kinds of different people together.

"After today you may work in pairs at each other's houses. Together you can decide on a project. Then you can present it at our Thinking Day party in two weeks. But I thought we could start off today by making friendship cards for one another to exchange on Thinking Day."

The girls got up from their circle and gathered around the lunch tables. Mrs. Q. plunked down a large pad of colored paper.

"On your cards, try to say how you feel about each girl...what makes her unique." Mrs. Q. looked from Brownie to Brownie. "Do you all know what unique means?"

Krissy A.'s hand shot up. "Not like anybody else in the world."

Mrs. Q. nodded. "That's right. Think about what makes each girl special...not like anybody else in the world."

Marsha raised her hand. "Oh, I know. Like Amy is double-jointed. She can bend her thumb all the way back to her wrist!"

"That is indeed a unique talent," said Mrs. Q. with a smile. "But maybe you want to think of something different for your friendship cards. More inside stuff—" Mrs. Q. tapped her heart, "—like being thoughtful or kind." Then she started passing out the pretty sheets of colored paper along with bottles of glue and markers.

Just looking at art supplies made Corrie's hands itch to get started. But Corrie sat back in her seat. She liked to think about art stuff a little before diving right in.

Corrie looked around at Marsha and Amy and Sarah, and all her other friends who were busy working away. She tried to think about the spirit of friendship, like Mrs. Q. had said. Corrie loved her friends. She really did. And that made her think of hearts. That was it—heart-shaped cards! But not just any old ones. Corrie wanted her heart cards to look special. Unique.

Corrie picked a piece of pale purple paper. Then, using just her fingers— no scissors—she tore out a heart. One side ended up much bigger than the other. And the point looked more like a tail. But Corrie liked her heart.

Marsha leaned over to look. "Ooh, Corrie. I never would have thought of that."

"Me neither," said Krissy A. quietly.

"That's because Corrie is a real *artiste*!" Amy said, making the word sound very French. "And someday rich people will pay a million dollars for a genuine, original Corrie."

Amy's words made Corrie flush with pleasure. Maybe she wasn't the world's best speller. But she did have an artistic nature. Mrs. Fujikawa had said so on her last progress report.

Corrie kept tearing out her paper hearts. But it was slow-going. By the time she was done, most of the other Brownies had already finished writing messages on their cards.

Mrs. Q. told Corrie she could do the writing part at home. And that was fine with Corrie. Spelling everything right was going to take her ages. Horrible old spelling! Why was it ever invented anyway?

*   *   *

At the very end of the meeting, after cleanup and the "Smile Song," Mrs. Q. came around with a Brownie beanie full of little slips of paper. "Please pick one," said Mrs. Q. "Each slip has a number. The person who gets the same number as you will be your partner for the Thinking Day project."

The girls all picked numbers. Corrie picked a three. "Are you a three?" she asked Amy. She hoped Amy was.

But no. Amy was a one.

"Are you a three?" she asked Marsha.

No. Marsha and Jo Ann were both fours. And Lauren and Sarah were twos.

"Corrie. I'm a three."

Corrie turned around. *¡Ay bendito!* Her partner was Krissy A. Corrie tried not to look disappointed. She didn't want to hurt Krissy's feelings. She wanted to feel the spirit of friendship. Still, Corrie figured Krissy was probably thinking the same thing that she was...Corrie and the Brain. What a pair!

2

That night after supper, Corrie practiced all her new spelling words. Twice!

Then she started writing out her friendship cards. Her mom sat nearby reading the paper, ready to help with the hard words.

Corrie read what she had just written about Amy. Corrie was sure most kids would write how Amy was "so much fun." And that was true. But Corrie wanted to write something special. Something only she could say. So, she had written, "Amy is special to me because when I tell her stuff, she always understands."

Corrie's card for Sarah seemed just right, too. "Sarah is special to me because she was my very first friend when I moved here last fall."

In fact, it was easy to write something about most of the girls in her troop. But when Corrie came to Krissy A., her mind went blank. All she could think of was "Krissy A. is special to me because she is so smart." That sounded weird. And it had nothing to do with the spirit of friendship. But it was so hard getting to know Krissy. Corrie never felt like her regular self around her. Sometimes she seemed more like a very short grown-up than a kid.

Corrie looked again at the empty heart with Krissy A.'s name on it. I'll do this one later, she thought, and put it back on the bottom of the pile.

Then Corrie looked over at her mom. "Is there any way to make yourself like somebody more?" Corrie took a breath. "Well, *like* isn't exactly what I mean. Is there any way to feel more like friends?"

Her mother looked up from the paper. "Well, spending more time together often helps. Then it happens all by itself."

"But what if that isn't working?" Corrie told her mom about having trouble with Krissy A.'s heart. And about being paired up with Krissy for the Thinking Day project.

"We shouldn't be partners. She's so smart."

"So are you!" said Corrie's mom.

"Oh right!" Corrie said. "You're my mother. You have to say that. It's like a rule."

Corrie's mom put down her paper. "No I don't. Listen. I know reading and spelling are still bumpy for you. But you are very bright. Reading was hard for me, too, at the beginning. And look at me now."

Corrie shrugged. It was true. Her mom read trillions of books and magazines. She was a reporter and, as she put it, lived by the printed word.

"Listen. Not everyone is going to be your best friend," her mom continued. "You'll find that some kids are just not your type, even if they are perfectly nice. And that's okay. Still, maybe with Krissy A., you just need to dig a little deeper. Investigate. You can have different kinds of friendships with different kinds of people. The trick is to find some common ground. Do you know what I mean?"

"I think so. You mean things you like to do together," Corrie said as she put her hearts away and got ready for bed. She thought about how she and Marsha loved to dress up and play with dolls. And how Lauren was teaching her how to play gin rummy.

Maybe Corrie could find some common ground with Krissy A., too. In any case, Corrie would have a chance tomorrow. She was going to Krissy's house to work on Thinking Day.

3

"Here we are!" Corrie's mom said cheerily the next morning. She had just pulled up in front of a big apartment building. Corrie spotted Krissy A. standing out front.

"Hi," Krissy said. "I waited down here for you, so your mom wouldn't have to find a parking space. Sometimes it's hard around here."

"Listen, sweetie, I should be done by about one," Corrie's mom told her as Corrie climbed out of the car. She was going to cover a story about a seventy-year-old man who had ridden a bike all the way across the United States. "As soon as the photographer is finished taking pictures, I'll be back to pick you up."

Corrie waved. Then she followed Krissy into the big building and onto an elevator with mirrored walls.

"Cool mirrors," said Corrie. She peered at the row after row of Corries reflecting back at her.

Krissy just nodded and looked straight ahead.

If Amy had been there, Corrie would have stuck out her tongue. Or made her eyes go all buggy. Just to see her weird face staring back at her millions of times. But with Krissy there, Corrie just stood and stared at the elevator door, too. She watched

the numbers light up above the door...16...
17...18...

Krissy A. licked her lips. She looked
like she was trying to think of something to
say but couldn't.

...27...28...Finally! They got off at the
top floor and went into Krissy's apartment.

Corrie followed Krissy down the hall to
her room. It didn't look at all like Corrie's
room, which had a dollhouse in one corner,
and a bed with about a hundred stuffed
animals on it. Krissy's room looked more
grown-up—almost like an office—with a
blue sofa instead of a regular bed, a desk
with a swivel chair, and bookshelves filled
with books.

"Wow! You have your own computer!"
Corrie said in surprise.

"Want to play a computer game?" Krissy
asked. She pointed to one on her desk. It

was called "Math Wizard." It looked hard and educational.

"Ummm, maybe later," Corrie said. She looked around the room. No dolls anywhere. No dress-up stuff. Not even any crayons or markers.

"I have an art program for the computer, too," Krissy went on. "You're so good in art. Maybe you'd like to try that."

Corrie almost said yes. But what if she got all mixed-up and couldn't understand the directions? She didn't want to look stupid in front of Krissy.

Corrie felt bad. She knew Krissy was trying to be nice. But Corrie shook her head. "Maybe later," she said again. "You want to try to think up something for Thinking Day?"

Krissy nodded quickly. She looked almost

relieved that they didn't have to try to have fun.

"I brought along my Brownie handbook," Corrie said.

"Oh, good," said Krissy. "I bet that'll give us an idea."

But after what seemed like a very long time, they still didn't know what to do. All they had decided was *not* to write a report on how Girl Scouts first started in England (Krissy's idea). And *not* to draw a big poster of the world with lots of foreign girls in pretty costumes holding hands (Corrie's idea).

They were getting nowhere fast! Corrie glanced at a clock in the shape of the moon on Krissy's wall. Yipes. It was only 11:23.

She hoped the bicycle man wasn't a big talker.

❊   ❊   ❊

"So what do you want to do now?" Krissy asked Corrie. There was a nervous edge to her voice. They had just finished a very quiet lunch of tunafish sandwiches.

"Should we try to think more about Thinking Day?" Krissy asked as she and Corrie walked back to her room.

Corrie shrugged. "I don't know. I guess. If that's what you want to do."

"I don't know either," Krissy said. Corrie thought she caught Krissy glancing at the moon clock now.

"Maybe—" both girls said at exactly the same time. Then they both giggled uncomfortably.

"You go first," Krissy said.

"No, you," Corrie said.

Just then the intercom sounded.

Saved by the buzzer!

"Corrie, your mother's waiting downstairs in the car for you," Krissy's dad called.

Corrie grabbed her handbook and headed down the hallway toward the front door. She thanked Krissy's parents for lunch. "And thanks for having me over," she said to Krissy.

"Sure." Krissy held the door open and smiled awkwardly. Corrie hoped Krissy couldn't tell that she was glad to be going. Anyway, Krissy looked kind of relieved, too. "Mmm...maybe I'll call you later if I get any ideas," she said.

Swoosh! The elevator door slid open.

"Sure. Well...bye." Corrie jumped into the elevator.

Swoosh! The door slid shut.

Corrie pushed the "L" button for Lobby. She made a face in the mirrors. It felt good to finally act silly. She pulled down her eyes and pushed up her nose. Ooh, gross! Her mother hated when she made that face.

The elevator stopped at another floor. Corrie quickly changed back to her normal face. An older woman in a jogging suit got on with a tiny dog. Her hair was as white and curly as her poodle's.

"Sit, Noodle," the woman said. But the little dog did not obey. Corrie laughed as it ran around and around her legs. Soon Corrie was all tangled up in the leash.

"Noodle, stop that!" said the woman. Then she unwound the leash.

"Sorry, sweetie," she told Corrie. Then she scooped up the dog and gave her a hug. "You're just too friendly for your own good!"

"That's okay," said Corrie. "I like dogs. But we can't get one because my mom's allergic."

"Oh, look, Noodle!" the woman exclaimed. She pointed to Corrie's handbook. "She's a Brownie! No wonder she's so friendly. I was a Brownie, too, when I was your age. Of course, that was centuries ago."

"No fooling!" said Corrie.

The woman laughed. "Well, not centuries exactly. But almost sixty years ago. I loved being a Brownie. I remember I joined a troop right after my family moved into a new town."

"Me too!" Corrie exclaimed.

The elevator stopped on the ground floor.

"Time for our jog now, Noodle Poodle." The woman put the dog down. "Well, it was nice talking to you. Have fun at Brownies."

As the woman jogged off, with Noodle trotting behind her, Corrie thought how weird it was. It had been easier talking to a woman she'd just met on an elevator than spending the morning with a girl she saw almost every day!

Corrie saw her mom's car and hopped into the backseat. Her older brother Rob was up in front.

"Did you have a nice time, honey?" her mom asked.

Corrie slunk back in the seat. "Not really. I don't know—I'm just not myself around Krissy. I always feel like I'm going to say something stupid. So I don't say anything. And Krissy *never* says much. So we both sat around not saying anything."

Corrie told her mom about not coming up with anything for their Thinking Day project. Then Corrie told about Noodle the Poodle and the woman on the elevator. "Can you believe it? She was once a Brownie too!"

Suddenly Corrie smacked herself in the head. "*¡Ay bendito!* I'm the dumbest person in the universe!"

"Not true," said her brother Rob. "You're not the dumbest person in the universe. You're just the dumbest person on Earth."

Corrie pretended she didn't hear him. Besides, maybe she wasn't so dumb anyway. Because she had just had a great idea. A brainstorm!

"That woman on the elevator. Maybe we could talk to her and find out what it was like being a Brownie back in the old days." Yes! It would be like a reporter doing an interview. Just like her mom.

What a great Thinking Day project!

"There is just one little problem," Corrie said, sinking back again in the car seat. "I have absolutely no idea who the woman is!"

As soon as she got home, Corrie called
Krissy A.

"Ooooh, yes! That's a really good idea."

Corrie felt a rush of pleasure at those
words. Then she described the woman on
the elevator. "Do you know who I'm
talking about?"

"Well, that could be a lot of people. Can
you tell me anything else about her?"

"Oh! I almost forgot!" said Corrie. "She
had a cute little poodle named—"

"Noodle!" Krissy A. chimed in. "I know

her. That's Mrs. Moser. She and my dad are on the recycling committee together. Hold on a second and I'll find out her number."

Soon Krissy was back on the phone with the number. "But, Corrie," Krissy paused. "Mmm...would you mind calling her?" Krissy sounded a little embarrassed.

"Sure," Corrie said, puzzled. "But you must know her better than I do."

"I guess," Krissy said. "But you'll be better at asking. I'm not good at that kind of stuff."

"No problem!"

So Corrie called the number. Mrs. Moser said she'd be delighted to help out fellow Brownies.

Then Corrie called Krissy back. It was all set for two o'clock the next day.

"Thanks, Corrie, for calling," Krissy said.

"It really is a great idea. You were so smart to think of it."

"Gee, thanks," Corrie said. Then she hung up and stared at the phone. Had Krissy the Brain just called Corrie smart?

And had they just had a real live conversation?

4

The next afternoon, Corrie met Krissy at her apartment. This time Corrie was looking forward to the visit. Kind of. It would be fun to talk to that woman—Mrs. Moser—again. And who knew? Maybe her mom was right after all. Maybe if she spent more time with Krissy, Corrie would feel more like they were friends. Maybe she could write something on Krissy's heart like "Krissy A. is special to me because we were Thinking Day partners." It wasn't great.

But it was something.

Corrie rang Krissy's bell, and the door opened right away.

"Hi," Krissy said.

She led Corrie into her room.

"I brought over my mom's tape recorder," Corrie told her. "We can be just like real reporters!" Then she showed Krissy what all the different buttons were for.

"I tried to think of some questions to ask Mrs. Moser," Krissy said to Corrie. "But I don't know if they're too boring." Krissy passed a notebook to Corrie. "I've never interviewed a real live person before." The way Krissy said "person," it sounded more like they were going to interview a Martian.

Corrie looked at all the questions written out in Krissy's neat handwriting. She could read a lot of the words. But not all of them.

Corrie looked at Krissy. Krissy was going to think she was really dumb. She could always say something like, "These are good questions. But I think I'll just ask stuff— you know—sort of spur of the moment." Then Corrie remembered her phone call with Krissy. Krissy had been too shy to call up Mrs. Moser. That was something Krissy couldn't do. And she had said so.

"Um, Krissy. I think I may need your help reading some of this." Corrie kept her eyes on the notebook pad.

"Sure," said Krissy. She acted like it was no big deal at all. "I'm not sure I spelled everything right anyway."

"Oh, right!" said Corrie, rolling her eyes.

And then, without even thinking about it, she reached over and gave Krissy a friendly bop on the head. "You and that big brain of yours!"

Krissy grinned. She didn't even seem to mind getting bopped. In fact, she seemed to like it. And Corrie liked her questions, especially the one asking if Mrs. Moser ever did naughty things when she was a kid. Corrie always wanted to know that about grown-ups.

Smiling, both girls left Krissy's room, Corrie with her tape recorder and Krissy with a camera. They were ready for their interview.

5

"Interview! Oh, I like the sound of that," Mrs. Moser said, holding Noodle and motioning the girls into her living room. "Somebody once said that everybody in the world gets to be famous for fifteen minutes. I guess my time is here!"

Corrie and Krissy sat down on the sofa. Mrs. Moser offered them mint tea in real china teacups with saucers, and cookies on a silver tray. It made Corrie feel very grown-up, and she tried her best not to spill.

"These cookies are so cute," said Corrie. They were in the shape of owls. Corrie bit the head off her owl. Mmm. They were good, too.

"I have an owl cookie cutter," Mrs. Moser explained. "My granddaughter gave it to me. You see, I'm just crazy about owls. I collect them."

"You do!" Corrie and Krissy said together.

"Not live ones, of course." Mrs. Moser waved a hand around her living room. "But wooden owls, glass owls, paintings of owls. You name it."

Corrie looked around the room. The harder she looked, the more owls she found.

It was like one of those hidden picture puzzles. There was an owl-shaped lamp on a table. Owl candlesticks over the fireplace. A wicker owl wastebasket. Mrs. Moser, Corrie noticed, even had on little silver owl earrings.

"How many owls do you have?" Krissy wanted to know.

"Oh, I lost track years ago. People give them to me for birthdays, holidays..." Mrs. Moser picked up a small white owl from the windowsill. "This is the first one I ever got. It's carved from soap. It was given to me by my Brownie troop leader."

"Ooh, excuse me," Corrie interrupted. "Could you hold on for a second? I forgot to turn on our tape recorder. This sounds really interesting."

Mrs. Moser waited while Corrie started the tape recorder.

"Now where was I? Oh yes—my troop leader," Mrs. Moser continued. "Troop leaders were called Brown Owls back in those days. And my Brown Owl—Miss Loftus was her name—made a soap owl for each girl when she flew up. I've kept it all these years and started a collection." Mrs. Moser shrugged and laughed. "I guess I just like the look of owls."

Mrs. Moser returned the soap owl to the windowsill. Then she picked up a photo album and sat down again on the sofa. "Last night I went through loads of old photos. And finally I found it—a picture of the whole troop." Mrs. Moser stopped at one page in the album. "Just promise me you won't laugh when you see us!"

Corrie and Krissy huddled close together so they could both get a good look at the picture. It was an old black-and-white photograph with one corner torn off. There were eight girls in the picture, four in front, sitting cross-legged on the ground, and four standing behind them. Next to the girls stood an older woman with an odd, broad-brimmed hat. The Brown Owl, Corrie figured.

"The girl standing on the left is me," Mrs. Moser said. "In full Brownie uniform. Very different, isn't it?"

The girls in the picture had on floppy caps, kind of like the ones the Seven Dwarfs wore in *Snow White*. And they were wearing dark, long-sleeved dresses with belts.

"That's Miss Loftus," Mrs. Moser said, pointing to the older woman. "The first thing we would do at every meeting was give a big hoot for our Brown Owl. I *loved* Miss Loftus. She was so nice to me. Very patient."

"Patient?" asked Corrie.

"Yes," Mrs. Moser replied. "I was not the world's easiest child. Oh, no. I loved being the center of attention. My maiden name was Swanson, and once I told everyone that my aunt was Gloria Swanson.

She was a big movie star back then. And oh, did I get myself into a terrible mess. Everyone wanted to meet 'Aunt Gloria' and get her autograph.

"Well, anyway, Miss Loftus helped me out of that jam. And she was the one who first encouraged me to be in skits and plays—to do something positive with my dramatic nature."

"And did you?" Krissy asked. Corrie noticed that Krissy had put her notebook of questions down and was looking more relaxed.

"Yes, I did," said Mrs. Moser. "I performed in front of an audience nearly every day for thirty-two years."

"You were an actress!" Corrie said.

"In a way," Mrs. Moser said with a smile. "I was a schoolteacher. I taught third graders. And believe me! You have to be an entertainer sometimes to keep an audience of eight-year-olds interested."

"I bet you were a wonderful teacher," said Krissy. "I want to be a teacher more than anything when I grow up. But I don't know if I'd be so good... I'm not much of an entertainer."

"It's not all that hard," Mrs. Moser assured her. "With kids, it always helps if you just let yourself act a little silly sometimes."

The girls spent an hour talking to Mrs. Moser. She showed them her old Brownie pin, which didn't look at all like Brownie pins now. But they also found that many things about Brownies hadn't really changed much. Mrs. Moser's troop had gone on camp-outs, just like Corrie and Krissy's troop. And Mrs. Moser's troop had planted a garden. Mrs. Q. was going to let their troop do that, too, once the weather got warmer. Why, Mrs. Moser's troop even used to sing the "Smile Song." And she proved it by singing it right into the tape recorder.

Mrs. Moser knew some other Brownie songs, too. Songs Corrie and Krissy had never heard before. One went like this:

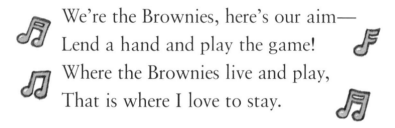

We're the Brownies, here's our aim—
Lend a hand and play the game!
Where the Brownies live and play,
That is where I love to stay.

Mrs. Moser even showed the girls photographs of her children and grandchildren. One picture showed them all by an old castle. Everyone was smiling and waving to the camera.

Corrie's mouth fell open. "I know that place! It's in San Juan. In Puerto Rico."

"That's right! I taught in Puerto Rico for a year. My family came down to visit me."

"No kidding! I go to Puerto Rico every summer!" Corrie exclaimed. "I've been to that mansion, *La Fortaleza*, many times."

"And do you speak Spanish?" Mrs. Moser asked Corrie in Spanish.

"*Sí. Yo hablo español.* Yes. I can speak Spanish," Corrie answered.

"Corrie, I didn't know you could speak another language!" Krissy said. She sounded surprised—and impressed. "That's so cool!"

Corrie shrugged. It was no big deal really. "My mom is from Puerto Rico. And we go there every summer," she explained. "*Abuelo*—my grandpa—doesn't speak much English. So I kind of learned without even thinking about it."

Mrs. Moser showed the girls pictures of other places she'd been in Puerto Rico.

"Oh, I almost forgot," said Krissy. "We wanted to take pictures of you!"

So Krissy and Corrie took lots of pictures of Mrs. Moser. Then they thanked her for a wonderful interview. She gave them each another Brown Owl cookie, for the road.

"*¡Adiós!*" called Mrs. Moser, waving to the girls as they headed to the elevator.

"*¡Adiós!*" Krissy chimed in with Corrie.

6

Once they were back in Krissy's room, the girls turned on the tape recorder and listened to the interview. In the background they could hear Noodle yapping away now and then. Still, everybody's voice came out loud and clear.

"Ooh, do I really sound like that?" Corrie said, making a face.

"I was thinking the same thing. It sounds like I have a horrible cold!" said Krissy.

But all the Mrs. Moser stuff was really

interesting. It wasn't as interesting as hearing her in person, the girls agreed. But Corrie was sure the troop would like their project.

It was almost 4:30 by Krissy's moon clock. Krissy's dad had said he would drive Corrie home whenever she was ready.

"Want me to ask my dad if he'll take you home now?" Krissy asked awkwardly.

Corrie looked around the room. She was actually having a pretty good time. Maybe Krissy could teach her how to use the computer now. "Well...I'd like to stay. That is...if you want me to," Corrie added quickly.

"Sure!" Krissy looked surprised and very pleased. "I know! Want to teach me some Spanish?"

"*¡Sí!* That's 'yes.'" Corrie informed her.

And so the lesson began.

Corrie taught Krissy that *escuela* was "school." *Casa* was "house." And *amiga* meant "friend."

"*Amiga*," Krissy repeated. Then she looked at Corrie. "You're lucky, Corrie. You just moved here. And already you have lots of *amigas*. I've lived here forever. But part of me still feels like—" Krissy stopped for a moment, "—like a new kid." Krissy looked at Corrie. "Do you know what I mean?"

Corrie nodded. She did. But she never would have thought Krissy felt that way, too.

"I wish I were more like you," Krissy said softly.

"You do?"

"Why do you look so surprised?" Krissy asked.

"Well...it's just that...I was always

afraid that you thought I was—" Corrie paused, then spilled it out, "—not smart enough. I mean, you're such a brain. And you like such serious stuff."

"Serious stuff. Yep, that's me!" Krissy rolled her eyes and made a face. "My parents say that even when I was a baby, I was real quiet and serious. They say I always looked like I was trying to solve the problems of the world."

Corrie couldn't help giggling. "I'm not laughing at you, Krissy. Honest. I was just trying to picture you as a baby."

"Sometimes I wish I were—" Krissy looked like she was searching for the right word, "—sillier. That's it! Sillier."

Corrie didn't know what to say. She could help Krissy learn some Spanish. But she didn't see how she could help her learn to be sillier . . . or could she?

Corrie dug into her jeans pocket. She took out a roll of mints.

"Well, you are in luck. Because I happen to have, here with me, some Silly Pills." She handed one to Krissy.

Krissy popped the mint in her mouth. "Mmmm. Very good. I think it's starting to work already." Krissy looked at Corrie. "I don't want to learn regular Spanish anymore. Teach me silly Spanish!"

So Corrie did. She taught Krissy A. the words for "underwear" and "toilet" and "jellybeans." She even taught Krissy a whole sentence. *Estoy tan feliz mi amiga no tiene tres hoyitos en la nariz.* It meant, "I am glad my friend does not have three nostrils."

Before they knew it, Krissy's dad told them it was time to drive Corrie home.

They dropped Corrie off in front of her house. "*¡Adiós, amiga!*" Krissy called out.

"*¡Adiós, amiga!*" shouted Corrie.

Then all of a sudden, it hit her! She was feeling it—the spirit of friendship. Just like Mrs. Q. had said. Brownies really could bring very different kinds of people together.

7

On the Friday of the Thinking Day party, the Brownies set up their projects in the lunchroom. Mrs. Q. went around admiring them all. "Wonderful. Just wonderful," she kept on saying. "I can tell you all had on your thinking caps and put a lot of thought into Thinking Day." Then she asked each pair of girls to tell about their project.

Marsha and Jo Ann taught the troop songs and games from other countries. "In Thailand, Brownies are called Bluebirds," said Marsha. "And they like to play a game called *Takraw*. It's like Hacky Sack, only you use a wicker ball." Jo Ann demonstrated, then let each girl try.

Sarah and Lauren had had a Dog Wash Day. They had washed eleven dogs to raise money for the Juliette Low World Friendship Fund. "We used special dog shampoo and old hairbrushes," said Lauren. "They looked just like they were ready for a dog show!"

All the projects were different— "unique," Mrs. Q. said. The last group to present was Corrie and Krissy A.

"We talked to a woman who used to be a Brownie Girl Scout a long time ago," Corrie said. "We did an interview on a tape recorder and took lots of pictures."

"But then we thought that meeting the woman in person would be even better," Krissy went on.

"So!" Corrie waved to Mrs. Moser, who was sitting at one of the lunch tables. "Here she is, in living color. Mrs. Augusta Swanson Moser!"

The troop really liked Mrs. Moser. She brought a big tin of her owl cookies for everyone. And after the friendship squeeze,

Corrie gave Mrs. Moser a special owl picture she had made out of bits of torn paper. "This is for your collection," Corrie explained.

Just before the meeting ended, it was time to exchange friendship cards. There were lots of laughs and hugs as the girls read what they'd written about one another.

Krissy A. smiled and gave Corrie a folded-over card. It was white with gray computer-printed hearts all over the front.

Corrie picked up a pale purple heart and handed it to Krissy A. It had a squiggly line of silver glitter all around the edges.

Together they opened their cards and read them. Then they burst out laughing. They were supposed to be so different...weren't they? Then how come they'd written almost the same thing!

I like Corrie because she is my special new friend and ella no tiene tres hoyitos en la nariz.

I like Krissy A. because she is my newest friend, and ella no tiene tres hoyitos en la nariz.

Girl Scout Ways

Marsha and Jo Ann taught their troop games from other countries. Here's one you can play. It comes from the Philippines. The game is called Tapatan, and it's a lot like tic-tac-toe.

- Tapatan is for two players. Each player gets three moving pieces. Use checkers, beans, or anything! The object of the game is to make a row across, up and down, or diagonally.

- Draw this diagram on a piece of paper. The game is played on the nine points where the lines cross.

- Each player takes turns putting their pieces down on an empty point until all the pieces are on the game board.

- Once all the pieces are down, player one moves one piece along a line to the next empty point. Move up, down, across, or diagonally, but no jumping over pieces. Then player two does the same. Keep taking turns until someone makes a row of three.

 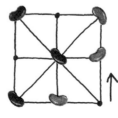